An Englishwoman is arrested for demonstrating in
front of the prime minister's house for the right to vote.

Cornerstones of Freedom

The Story of
THE WOMEN'S MOVEMENT

By Maureen Ash

℗ CHILDRENS PRESS®
CHICAGO

Old engraving shows a wife auction in England.

Cover and page 2—Suffragettes held parades
to attract supporters to their cause—the
vote for women.

PHOTO CREDITS

The Bettmann Archive—Cover, 8
Historical Pictures Service, Chicago—5, 10,
   11 (left), 12 (right), 15 (top left), 16 (right),
   18 (left), 19 (left)
Lake County Museum, Curt Teich Postcard
   Collection—19 (right), 20 (right)
Bettye Lane—28 (right)
National Portrait Gallery, London—13
Northwind Picture Archives—1, 2, 4, 6 (both
   photos), 9, 32
Photri—15 (top left), 15 (bottom right), 17,
   26 (left), 30
Sophia Smith Collection, Smith College—11
   (right), 16 (left)
TSW-Click/Chicago:
   © Billy Barnes—23 (right), 24
Wide World Photos—3, 12 (left), 18 (right),
   20 (left), 23 (left), 27, 28 (left), 31
Karen Yops—26 (right)

Library of Congress Cataloging-in-Publication Data

Ash, Maureen.
   The story of the women's movement / by Maureen Ash.
      p.   c. — (Cornerstones of freedom)
   Summary: A brief history of how women in this country
have tried to gain equal rights with men.
   ISBN 0-516-04724-8
   1. Women's rights—United States—History—
Juvenile literature.   2. Feminism—United States—
History—Juvenile literature. [1. Women's rights—
History. 2. Feminism—History.] I. Title.
II. Series.
HQ1236.5.U6A76   1989   89-17325
305.42'0973—dc20   CIP
                                                AC

Caroline
Sheridan
Norton

A little more than a hundred years ago women in England and America did not have the right to own property, keep the money they earned, vote, get an education, or get custody of their children. Each of these rights was won through the efforts and sacrifices of some extraordinary women.

Caroline Sheridan Norton lived in England. In 1827, she married George Norton, a lawyer. Until their marriage, he had seemed sober and dependable. She was to find out that he was often drunk and had a violent temper. He beat her, even when she was pregnant. Under the law, he could treat Caroline as he wished. She could do nothing to stop him.

George and Caroline Norton had three boys. The youngest child was two when George, jealous because Caroline was becoming a successful writer, took the children away. He would not allow her to see them. Caroline asked for legal help but found that George was completely within his rights. As a married woman, Caroline had no legal existence. She could not even ask a court for a hearing in her case.

Caroline fought to get her children back. She wrote letters to anyone she thought might help. She wrote a pamphlet attacking the law that gave her children away. At the same time, she tried to support herself through her writing. Her books and plays were successful, but legally, a married woman's earnings went to her husband. George got the money Caroline earned. Caroline tried to change this law, too.

Although women worked in coal mines (left) and as dressmakers (right), the money they earned belonged to their husbands.

The Infants Custody Bill was passed in 1839. It allowed a mother to keep her children under the age of seven if other conditions were met. Caroline had worked to get this bill passed, but the new law could not help her. George had taken her children to Scotland, where the law did not affect them.

Some people sympathized with Caroline, but many thought she was a terrible person. Women were supposed to be quiet and meek. Caroline was neither. She was talkative and a fighter. She continued to fight to regain her children and to keep the money she earned.

Caroline never regained custody of her sons. After her youngest child, eight-year-old William, died of blood poisoning, George allowed Caroline to keep their older boys with her for half the year. He could, however, order them to leave her at any time, for as long as he wished, and he did this often.

A bill that allowed married women deserted by their husbands to keep their earnings was passed in 1857. Caroline Norton died in 1877. In 1882, a law that gave married women the same rights as unmarried women (though not the same rights as men!) was passed.

One reason men had made laws such as the ones Caroline Norton worked to change was that men believed themselves to be smarter than women.

An 1871 drawing showing Englishwomen attending a sewing circle

Over the years it was sometimes pointed out to them that women might seem more capable if they were allowed to get the same education that men received. It was not until Emily Davies began to fight for the education of women that girls got the chance to learn more.

Emily Davies was born in 1830 in Southampton, England. Her father was a poor clergyman. Emily had lessons with her brothers and enjoyed them, but at that time only boys went to college.

At girls' schools, young women learned to play the piano, do needlepoint, speak a little French, and move gracefully. Girls did not learn science, mathemetics, or literature. Only boys did.

As Emily grew older, she hungered to learn more and eagerly attended public lectures whenever and wherever she could. She met other women who also wanted a better education. Emily decided to do something about it. Over the years she wrote letters and formed societies promoting education for women. She discovered that of the 320 trades and professions open to men, not one was open to women. Women were expected to get married and have children and do nothing else with their lives.

Emily found that some people felt that classes for girls should be easier than those for boys. Girls were too weak, it was believed, to learn mathematics—it would make them go mad.

A cooking class held in a school for young women

Male professors taught many of the subjects at Girton College.

Emily disagreed. She opened Girton College for women. The young women attending Girton had to live up to the same educational standards as men.

When Emily Davies was born, there were four universities in England, none of them open to women. By the time she died, in 1921, there were twelve universities, all open to women. Much of this progress was due to the work of Emily Davies and the women she inspired.

Caroline Norton and Emily Davies lived in England. Though the United States had won its independence from England, it was still influenced by English custom and laws. Married women had no legal existence and could not keep their wages or own property.

Molly Pitcher (left) fought in the Battle of Monmouth in 1778. The executive committee of the Pennsylvania Antislavery Society, in 1851, included women. Lucretia Mott is sitting in the front row, second from the right.

American women worked hard—during the Revolution they had woven cloth for themselves and their families to avoid buying silk and linen from England, and many women had disguised themselves as men and fought in the war against England. Even so, when the United States Constitution was adopted in 1789, it did not include women, or black men, or native Americans.

It was through working to end the slavery of black people in America that women learned to work for themselves. Antislavery societies began to form in the 1830s, and women began to speak in public for the rights of black people. The women's antislavery societies sent so many petitions to Congress to end

Elizabeth Cady Stanton

Lucretia Mott

slavery that a law was introduced to make it illegal for a woman to petition Congress. Fortunately the law did not pass.

It soon became clear to women that they needed what men had, the right to vote. One woman who devoted her life to working for women's suffrage (the right to vote) was Elizabeth Cady Stanton.

Elizabeth Cady was the daughter of a judge. She watched women come to her father with worried faces. They often left in tears. Once she heard a woman telling Judge Cady that her drunken husband was going to sell the farm her parents had left to her. Judge Cady told the woman that her husband was within his rights. He owned all the property, and she could do nothing to stop him. Married women had no legal existence.

Elizabeth tried to cut the unfair law from her father's book with scissors but was stopped. She was intelligent and strong willed, and later put these qualities to work in her fight against slavery, and for the rights of women.

Elizabeth married Henry Stanton, and they went to England as delegates to an antislavery convention. At the convention, Elizabeth found that women delegates were not only denied the right to speak, they had to sit behind curtains and could not even watch the proceedings. Elizabeth could not believe that women could be treated like that. She met Lucretia Mott, a woman who was also outraged about the situation. They decided to hold a convention in the United States, demanding rights for women.

The 1840 convention of the World Anti-Slavery Society met in London, England. Women attended the convention, but they had to sit behind curtains and were not allowed to speak at the meeting.

Eight years later in 1848, the Seneca Falls Convention took place. Elizabeth Cady Stanton, Lucretia Mott, and several other women presented a Declaration of Sentiments, which was modeled after the Declaration of Independence. One of the resolutions called for women's right to vote. The declaration was supported by most of the 300 women and men at the convention, though many newspapers made fun of the event.

Elizabeth also became friends with Susan B. Anthony. The two friends organized more conventions and wrote speeches and letters. In 1860, thanks to the work of Susan B. Anthony, Elizabeth Cady Stanton, and many others, the New York Assembly passed the Married Woman's Property Act. Now a married woman controlled both her property and her wages. This law became the model for similar laws passed by other states.

During the Civil War most of the people who had been active in the women's movement worked for the Union cause. At the end of the war, the Thirteenth Amendment was passed, which ended slavery. Then the Fourteenth Amendment was passed. The feminists were bitterly disappointed with its wording. It stated clearly that voting was only for males. Elizabeth Cady Stanton and Susan B. Anthony and other feminists had to start over.

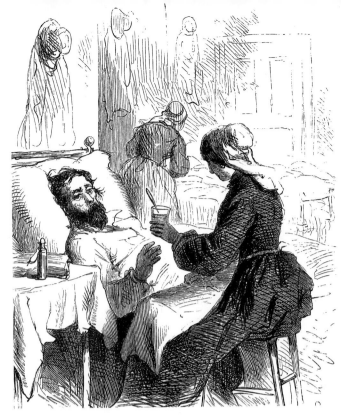

Susan B. Anthony (above left). During the Civil War, women worked in factories and hospitals. When the war ended they renewed their efforts to get Congress to grant women the right to vote (below right).

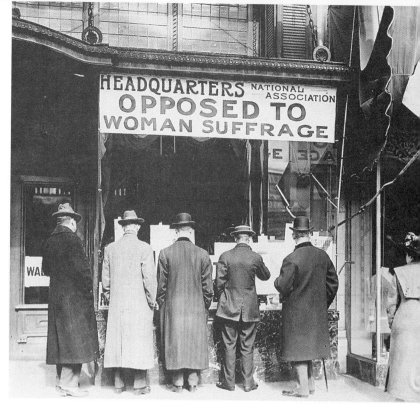

Copy of *The Revolution* (left) published on January 6, 1870. The National Anti-Suffrage Association (right) was organized to fight the women's movement.

Elizabeth and Susan started a newspaper called *The Revolution*. Elizabeth had seven children and had previously worked at home, writing speeches and articles. Now her youngest was ten years old and she felt able to travel about the country, lecturing on women's suffrage. She grew used to being ridiculed and even having rotten eggs and vegetables thrown at her. Elizabeth and others continued to work for women's rights. In the 1870s an amendment giving women the vote was introduced to Congress. It was voted down in 1878.

Elizabeth Cady Stanton died in 1902. Susan B. Anthony died in 1906. They left behind a strong

Women's suffrage parade held in Washington, D. C., in 1907

organization. After a great deal of effort by thousands of women, the Nineteenth Amendment, which gave women the vote, was passed in 1920.

The women who worked to win the vote believed that women would use the vote to change unfair laws. They would vote for officials who supported ideas such as equal pay for equal work. People who were against women's suffrage thought women would use the vote to become too powerful. Both sides were wrong.

Women tended to vote as their husbands voted. Because they had the vote, women felt that they had all the rights they needed. They felt they had come as far as they could, and the women's movement faded.

17

During the 1930s, laws were passed against hiring married women (left). Women continued to work for causes, such as the anti-alcohol movement (above).

During the 1930s, a time most people call the Great Depression, twenty-six states passed laws against hiring married women. People thought that women didn't really need to work if they had husbands. The lawmakers apparently didn't think about the women married to men who could not or would not hold jobs, or the women with large families who worked to help their husbands pay for rent and food and clothing. For the same work, it was common to pay a man higher wages than a woman simply because he was a man.

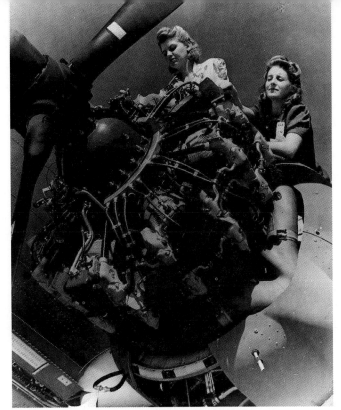 

During World War II, women worked in factories (left) and did many other jobs that once were done by men. After the war, these jobs were not offered to women. Most advertisements (right) showed women working at home—not in offices or factories.

During World War II millions of men went off to fight. Women took their places in the factories, and they kept the country running. When the war was over, a curious thing happened. The women were fired. They were told that factory work was too hard. The women found other low-paying jobs, as waitresses, secretaries, and as unskilled workers. Women's work outside the home was treated as less valuable. Only the work they did in their homes was considered meaningful.

A book was published in 1963 that changed the way people thought about women in America. It was

Betty Friedan (right) did not believe that all the mothers that stayed home were contented and happy.

called *The Feminine Mystique.* Its author, Betty Friedan, had noticed that the women she knew were not like the contented women she saw on television shows. The housewives she talked to were tired and depressed. They were good wives and good mothers and kept their homes clean, but Friedan found that they were quietly asking themselves, "Is this all there is to my life?"

Betty Friedan studied labor statistics. She found that half of all adult women were working forty hours a week outside the home. In 1950, a woman's average wage was 65 percent of a man's. And there were almost no women in politics, or at the executive level in business, or in professions such as the law and medicine.

The Feminine Mystique made women think about the way they were treated. At the same time, black people were protesting the way they were treated. And students began to protest the war in Vietnam.

In 1964 a civil rights bill came before Congress. Part of it was called Title VII, and it outlawed job discrimination by employers on the basis of "race, color, religion, or national origin." In an effort to defeat the bill, some southern representatives added the word "sex" to the bill. They thought this would make the bill a joke, and it would be voted down. Most of the men in the House of Representatives did laugh over the way the bill had been changed, but Representative Martha Griffiths of Michigan didn't. She insisted that the word "sex" be left in. And when the bill went to the Senate, Senator Margaret Chase Smith of Maine would not let the word be taken out. And the bill passed.

In 1966, Betty Friedan and other women formed the National Organization for Women. NOW kept its eyes on how the new civil rights act was enforced. At first the Equal Employment Opportunity Commission did not seem to care about enforcing the law with respect to women. NOW forced the EEOC to do its job.

The new law had one of its first tests when female flight attendants complained that they were being forced to quit when they got married or when they turned thirty or thirty-five. NOW helped the attendants organize. They won their case! The law had another test when NOW pointed out that newspapers still ran "Help Wanted" ads under two headings: "Help Wanted—Female" and "Help Wanted—Male." NOW pressured the EEOC into making the newspapers run their ads alphabetically, as Title VII required, without listing the jobs as available only to men or only to women.

At first, the women's movement of the sixties didn't attract many young women. They were concerned with civil rights for black people and with the protest against the Vietnam War. But when the Students for a Democratic Society, one of the most active student groups, took over the administration building at Columbia University in 1968, the men told the women to make spaghetti for them while they thought up things to do next. The women protested but the men wouldn't listen. Because of this and other incidents like it, the women's movement gained many new, young members.

The movement became more and more powerful. Politicians could no longer count on women voting for the same people as their husbands did. Women everywhere began to notice discrimination and to work against it. On August 26, 1970, the fiftieth

The National Organization for Women continues to support equal rights demonstrations. Buttons and bumper stickers are used to carry the feminist message to others.

anniversary of the day women won the right to vote in the United States, thousands of women went on strike. In New York City alone, between 35,000 and 50,000 women marched down Fifth Avenue, bringing traffic to a halt. They were honoring the early feminists and calling attention to the ways in which women were still not treated fairly.

It was unfortunate but true that women were still not being treated fairly. Back in 1923, after women had won the vote, an amendment had been proposed to the Constitution. It stated that "Men and women shall have equal rights throughout the United States and every place in its jurisdiction." This was called

Equal rights rally in North Carolina

the Equal Rights Amendment. It was proposed to each session of Congress after that and was voted down every time. Finally, in 1971, the Equal Rights Amendment was passed by Congress. To become law, it had to be ratified, or voted on and passed, by thirty-eight states. Congress allowed the states seven years to vote on the amendment. If thirty-eight states had not passed it by 1979, it would die.

This is the wording of the Equal Rights Amendment that went out to the states in 1972.

Section 1. Equality of rights under the law shall not be denied or abridged by the United States or by any state on account of sex.

Section 2. The Congress shall have the power to enforce, by appropriate legislation, the provisions of this article.

Section 3. This amendment shall take effect two years after the date of ratification.

Some people wondered why women needed such an amendment. The Civil Rights Act of 1964 protected them from discrimination in employment.

Supporters of the ERA pointed out that for every dollar a man earned in the early 1970s, a woman earned only fifty-eight cents. An article in *Time* magazine pointed out that for a woman to earn more than a man with an eighth-grade education, she needed a college degree. The United States Census Bureau listed 441 occupations in a job survey. It was found that most women were in the 20 lowest-paid classifications. Black women were the lowest-paid of all. Because an amendment to the Constitution overrides all local, state, and federal laws, ERA supporters felt that it would provide the best basis for economic change for women. Laws did exist to provide equal opportunity for women, but these varied from state to state and could change with the next set of lawmakers.

In 1975 the U.S. Commission on Civil Rights pointed out that the government itself was not making an effort to enforce its equal opportunity laws. The ERA's supporters believed that the ERA would pressure government administrators into enforcing laws that prevented unfair practices.

Countless demonstrations were held in support of the ERA.

The ERA had to be ratified, or voted on and passed, by thirty-eight states by March, 1979. Within one year after Congress voted to submit it to the states, thirty state legislatures approved it. Everyone felt that the amendment would become part of the U.S. Constitution. But they were wrong.

The ERA had not been ratified by March, 1979, so Congress granted an additional thirty-nine months for undecided states to vote on it. By this time, organized opposition to the ERA had come into force.

Many people opposed to the ERA felt that they did not want the Supreme Court and federal agencies making decisions about equal rights. They wanted those decisions made by their own states and local governments, where they felt their voices could be better heard. And many people opposed the ERA because they didn't want social customs to change. They liked the idea of definite "masculine" and "feminine" roles. They were afraid there would no longer be separate public bathrooms for men and women. They were afraid divorced men would no longer be required to support their families. And they were afraid that women would be drafted.

Supporters of the ERA tried to dispel these fears. The ERA would not change social customs. Public bathrooms would remain separate. Courts would probably rule that the parent most able to support his or her family should do so in case of divorce, or that they should share in the responsibility. And women might very well be drafted.

The idea of women serving in the military frightened many people. A report by the *Yale Law Review* said that the ERA would require that

Many women did not support the ERA.

Phyllis Schlafly (left) led the opposition against the Equal Rights Amendment. The ERA supporters (right) lost.

women participate in military service on the same basis as men. They would also have the same exemptions, or excuses not to serve. Under a draft, men with dependent children or other special responsibilities don't have to join the service, and women with those responsibilities wouldn't, either.

Few women were happy about the military service part of the ERA, but most supporters saw that gaining full equality with men meant making the same sacrifices, too.

All the same, many people remained afraid of the changes they thought the ERA would allow. Opponents of the ERA emphasized these fears, and no one was better at doing so than Phyllis Schlafly, a married woman and mother of six children. Mrs. Schlafly wasn't the only one who opposed the ERA. But even ERA supporters said that if Mrs. Schlafly had been on their side, the ERA would have passed.

Mrs. Schlafly founded the Eagle Forum. It was, she said, a group for women who were not interested in women's liberation. She published a newsletter, spoke on the radio, wrote a newspaper column, and earned a law degree as she fought against the ERA. She formed Stop-ERA groups in every state.

Mrs. Schlafly felt that the ERA was dangerous and would take away more rights than it would bestow. She said that the women's movement made a woman's role as a homemaker and mother seem degrading. She did not want women to be drafted.

Mrs. Schlafly was a good speaker. She had a good sense of humor and was cool under pressure. People liked her. She was an excellent leader, and her fight to stop the ERA was successful. Only thirty-five states had ratified the ERA by June 30, 1982, the deadline Congress had set. The ERA was dead.

The ERA has been introduced to Congress at every session since then, but has always been voted down. All the same, women have been making progress.

The Equal Rights Amendment may still become part of our Constitution one day. In the meantime, both sexes are more free to be as they wish. Both men and women are benefiting from their new right to choose.

Women, however, must struggle for equality even today—and probably tomorrow. There are 435 members of the United States House of Representatives, and only 25 are women. There are 100 senators in the United States Senate, and only 2 are women. For every dollar a man earned in 1987, a woman earned seventy cents. A woman with a college education still earns less, on the average, than a male high-school dropout. Fifty-seven percent of the households headed by women in this country are poor. Being poor reduces a person's opportunities to choose.

The right to choose is what the women's movement has always been about. Feminists don't believe that they are better than men, nor do they dislike men. The women who have worked for equal rights believe that men and women are just that—equal. Every man and every woman deserves to be treated fairly and deserves to be able to choose and work for what he or she wants in life. As Betty Friedan said in 1968, "We can say with absolute assurance that we do not speak for every woman in America, but we speak for the *right* of every woman in America to become all she is capable of becoming—in her own right and/or in partnership with men."

Pro-ERA demonstrations are still held.

INDEX

About the Author

Maureen Ash grew up riding horses and reading books in Milaca, Minnesota. She likes
cross-country skiing, swimming, and roller blading. She has a blue house, a big garden,
a small daughter, and a long, narrow cat.